For Stephen Gammell,
an inspiring Master of the Magic.
—K.A.

And for my friend Cynthia Rylant,
whose work is Magic.
—B.M.

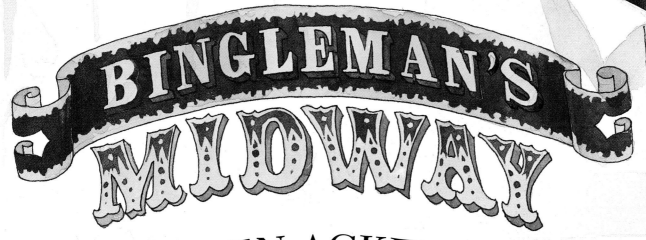

BINGLEMAN'S MIDWAY

BY KAREN ACKERMAN

ILLUSTRATED BY BARRY MOSER

BOYDS MILLS PRESS

MERRILL MEMORIAL LIBRARY 1904 YARMOUTH, ME.

In MIDSUMMER, THE VIEW FROM OUR FARMHOUSE porch on Route 6 in Ohio changed in the few hours between sun-up and late morning. It was a difference you could hear as well as see.

The sun turned from pale to deep yellow as the cool, silvery quiet of dawn slipped away, and by ten A.M. there was a wild music of crickets and dragonflies humming, and crows cawing and flapping over our fields of corn and soybeans. Now and then we could hear a neighbor's new and mysterious television set blaring.

Through this natural clatter, we first heard Bingleman, as did our neighbors—some of whom slowly moseyed outside to see what the ruckus was about.

Bingleman stood atop the first of six run-down trucks lined up on the Route, each one loaded with oddly shaped things covered in colored tarps. He wore a patchwork vest over a wrinkled shirt with the cuffs rolled up, and a pair of breeches that ballooned at the sides

before narrowing into his scuffed brown boots. A cap was turned sideways on his thick, wavy hair.

He was clearly not from Ohio.

We followed Pa out of the house to the roadside, though most of our neighbors stayed put on their porches, happy to let Pa do the inquiring.

"Name's McKinney. Got trouble here?" Pa called up to the man scowling down from the truck-top.

By this time, several other people had climbed out of the line of trucks and were walking toward Bingleman, nearly all of them shaking their heads and laughing. Some were speaking foreign-sounding words we didn't understand.

"You want to know what trouble is?" Bingleman snapped. "Trouble is a bunch of no-good-niks too lazy to work for a day's wages in Bingleman's Midway!" he replied and waved his arms at the others.

Suddenly there was a loud crack, and the truck on which Bingleman stood crashed downward. Pointing to the flattened tire,

Bingleman crowed, "See what I mean?" But he seemed to address the sky rather than Pa.

"I'll help you with that," Pa volunteered, stepping up to the disabled wheel.

"Nosir!" the Midway man shouted. "Not when I'm paying this sorry crew good money!" He drew a breath to calm himself and then hollered, "Where's Kodak?"

Kodak must've been asleep in one of the trucks, as when he appeared, his hair was all at angles and he was rubbing his eyes with both fists.

"Ri-cheer, Mr. Bingleman," Kodak muttered. "I'm on it."

While Kodak fixed the flat, Pa invited Bingleman into the house. Nathaniel and I were astonished, recalling all of Pa's lectures on keeping our distance from strangers.

We trailed after them to the kitchen. "Get our guest a cup, Drew," Pa instructed me, which I did, and Pa poured him some dark, boiled coffee from the pot.

"Where're you headed?" Pa asked politely, leaning back in his

chair casual-like. I was surprised, since he was usually less relaxed with folks he didn't know.

"Anywhere there's space to set up," Bingleman said. "Folks come, no matter where. Can't help it." Then, with a low chuckle, he teased, "Midway magic's hard to resist."

Nathaniel's mouth was open so wide I could see the new filling, shiny as a silver dollar, in his back tooth.

"Buncha guff," I muttered, not entirely under my breath.

Bingleman emptied his cup in one swallow and set it down on the tabletop. "Thanks for your hospitality, Mr. McKinney," he said and stood up to leave. "You be sure to bring your boys round for a look-see," he added with a laugh, and he gave me a grin and side-glance that brought the hairs on the back of my neck up in shivers.

Bingleman left the house, walked to the Route, and hopped into the repaired lead truck. All at once the engines started and the caravan began to move. The neighbors and their kids gathered around the line of trucks, and their curiosity wasn't wasted by Bingleman. As the trucks rolled away, he leaned out the window

and hawked, with a slash of his cap through the air, "Don'tcha forget—Bingleman's Midway is a once-a-life somethin' to see!"

Then he was gone, lost in the dust rising from the spin of near-bald truck tires.

"Can we, Pa?" Nathaniel whined. "Please, please, can we go?" all the while tugging everywhere at Pa's sleeves and pant legs.

"Hush, now!" Pa scolded. "We'll just see. You finish your chores, Drew?" he asked me.

"Yessir!" I replied, with a wink to Nathaniel. He was my little brother, and I wanted him to be happy.

"Well, then, we'll just see."

But Pa seemed to forget all about Bingleman's Midway for the rest of the night, though Nathaniel jabbered of nothing else till he fell asleep in the lower bunk.

"It's just a dumb carnival, Nate!" I advised. "Old-time tricks, raggy tents, and broken-down trucks!"

"But it's a MIDWAY, Drew!" Nathaniel sleepily answered. "A REAL midway!" he sighed and then was silent.

"Buncha guff," I growled and fell asleep, too.

Sure enough, Nathaniel started in on Pa first thing in the morning, and finally Pa gave in. We were going to see Bingleman's Midway that very afternoon.

At last the chores were done. We got washed, put on clean clothes, and the three of us set off down the Route. Pa seemed to know exactly where Bingleman would be.

When we came up on the fallow clearing called Coplan's Field where Bingleman had indeed found his "space," the sight of the brightly colored tents was downright startling against the green grass. The field was full of folks, so Bingleman was right about them not resisting.

"Keep an eye out for your brother, Drew," Pa told me, and I nodded.

All the trucks had disappeared, likely behind the two parallel rows of tents. And then we saw Bingleman.

His breeches and shirt had been pressed crisp, his scuffy boots polished to a shine, and his patchwork vest replaced with a fancy black one. He wore a wide-brimmed felt hat and barked into a golden megaphone.

"Come one, come all!" he told the crowd. "See the one and only Bingleman's Midway with all its miracles and magic! Guaranteed to mesmerize the eyes and stupefy the senses!"

"Buncha guff!" I snorted.

"Wow-ee!" Nathaniel said, open-mouthed again.

But Pa was quiet and had a strange look on his face.

Bingleman saw us and gave us a wink as we strode down the midway created by the tent rows. Nate strained to get a peek into each tent, but Pa hauled him back. "I'll decide what you see or don't, son," he said softly.

There was a lot to see.

Pa let us see it all. But when we got to the magic-show tent, he stopped cold.

"Come on, Pa!" Nate groaned, pulling him.

For some reason, Pa looked over at me, and I got another one of those shivers up my neck. But he led us inside, and we found three empty folding chairs to sit in.

Still, Pa kept looking at me.

"You awright, Drew?" he asked, almost in a whisper.

"Buncha guff!" I hissed with a nod.

But he must've known all along what might happen, because when the tent went dark and the spotlights came up, the air in my windpipe was caught short and high.

Bingleman stood in a single spotlight, dressed in a black cape, silk top hat, satin shirt, and bow tie. Behind him trotted a young woman in a short, sparkly red costume, holding a leopard by a chain leash.

He sawed that woman right in half, and he put his head in the leopard's open jaws. He plucked watches and wallets out of folks' pockets on the sly, and pulled two white doves out of one lady's carpetbag as her husband grinned at him.

He took apart three connected rings with no breaks in them and then just slipped the rings back together, all in a flash. And he had a little box with a silver lock and key where he made coins vanish and reappear, while the crowd howled with laughter. I'd never seen anything so wonderful in my whole life.

I'd never imagined doing anything other than growing up and running Pa's farm, but right then I could see myself in Bingleman's place. I could feel the satin shirt against my skin, and the heat of the spotlight above.

Midway magic got to me, after all.

I remember Pa staring at me, and Nathaniel gawking, and then walking home at sundown in a kind of daze. Next thing I knew, it was pitch-dark, and I was creeping out of the house with a paper bag full of clothes, headed for Coplan's Field.

Bingleman caught me when I tripped over a tent support rope. He wore dingy long johns and boots, but his thick wavy hair was missing from his head.

"Well, well!" Bingleman harrumphed. "If it isn't 'Mr. Buncha-Guff'!" he said with a laugh, helping me to my feet. "Something tells me your Pa won't be surprised," he chuckled as I followed him to the Coplan house to use the telephone.

When Pa fetched me, he didn't holler. He picked up the paper bag of clothes in one hand and took me by the other. "I'm beholdin', Mr. Bingleman," he murmured, and we went down the road leading homeward.

Bingleman smiled and pretended to tip his top hat, going back into his trailer with a wink and a nod to the starry skies.

Pa said nothing for quite a ways. I almost couldn't stand it. "Aren't you gonna ask me why I ran off?" I finally pleaded, but he just shook his head and kept on walking.

When we got home, Pa led me to the door of the bedroom I shared with my younger brother, whose peaceful snores we could hear from the hallway. As much as Nate had liked Bingleman's Midway, it hadn't gotten to him like it had me. Standing there while he slept, I felt foolish—and even jealous of his easy dreams.

"I'm sorry, Pa," I whispered at the door. "I don't know why I did it," which was the truth.

Pa looked down and smiled. "When I was near your age, I was gone for almost two weeks before your grandpa caught up to me," he confessed. He gave me a pat on the head, and sent me in to bed.

It was a while before I heard the whole story of how Pa had once run off to join a midway. It was a lot longer before my memories of Bingleman began to fade.

I finally ran the family farm, just as Pa (and I) had always expected me to. My wife, Ellen, and I have two children, Eben and Maggie, and we all share a special feeling about farming, Route 6, and traveling carnivals.

And sometimes, late in the morning, when nature is making its midsummer racket across our fields of corn and soybeans, I find myself drawn out to the porch.

I stare over the tips of our crops, and without any real reason, my family is suddenly beside me. Together we look out to Route 6, each one of us quietly hoping to see a sudden trail of dust from near-bald truck tires, and to hear the sound of midway magic coming our way.

Text copyright © 1995 by Karen Ackerman
Illustrations copyright © 1995 by Barry Moser
All rights reserved

Published by Caroline House
Boyds Mills Press, Inc.
A Highlights Company
815 Church Street
Honesdale, Pennsylvania 18431
Printed in Mexico

Publisher Cataloging-in-Publication Data
Ackerman, Karen.
    Bingleman's midway / by Karen Ackerman ; illustrated by Barry Moser. —1st ed.
[32]p. : col. ill. ;   cm.
Summary : The story of a young boy who cannot resist the lure of a carnival when it visits
his small midwestern town.
ISBN 1-56397-366-9
1. Carnivals—Fiction—Juvenile literature. [1. Carnivals—Fiction.] Fairs--Fiction
I. Moser, Barry, ill. II. Title.
    [E]   1995
Library of Congress Catalog Card Number 94-79154   CIP

First edition, 1995
Book designed by Barry Moser
The text of this book is set in 15-point Galliard, designed by Matthew Carter in 1978.
The illustrations are done in transparent watercolor on paper handmade in 1982 by Simon Green.
The illustrator wishes to thank Cara Moser, Mrs. Pat Keith, and Travis and Jesse Keith for
their invaluable help and assistance.
Distributed by St. Martin's Press

10 9 8 7 6 5 4 3 2

Bingleman's midway
Askerman, Karen   60866

Merrill Memorial Library

DATE DUE

AU 25			
A 2			
OC			
NO 0			
AUG			
JU			
JU 2			
G A			
GAYLORD 234			PRINTED IN U. S.